This book belongs to

· ·

For Ingrid Selberg, with affection and admiration

Dorling  Kindersley

LONDON, NEW YORK, SYDNEY, DELHI, PARIS,
MUNICH, and JOHANNESBURG

First published in Great Britain in 2000 by
Dorling Kindersley Limited. 9 Henrietta Street,
Covent Garden, London WC2E 8PS

This paperback edition published in 2000

2 4 6 8 10 9 7 5 3 1

ISBN 0-7513-6384-7

A CIP catalogue record for this book is available from the British Library.

Colour reproduction by Dot Gradations, UK
Printed and bound in Malaysia by Tien Wah Press

see our complete
catalogue at
www.dk.com

Parsnip
and the **Pink Blanket**

A Lift-the-Flap Book by Sue Porter

A Dorling Kindersley Book

This is Parsnip's friend Blanket.
And this is Blanket's very soft and
cuddly pink blanket. She takes it
everywhere.

When she goes
out to play . . .

Yum!
Yum!

Whee!

When she eats
her supper . . .

and especially when she snuggles
down to sleep.

One day, Blanket was
busy eating when three naughty
kittens came by looking for fun.

Soon Parsnip, Champy, and
Tadpole came by to play with
Blanket. They heard a strange
noise from behind the hedge.

"My pink blanket has gone!"
sniffed Blanket.
"Don't be sad," said Parsnip.
"We'll help you find it."

They looked in the rabbit hutch . . .

They looked in the chicken coop . . .

and they looked in
the farmer's van . . .

No one had seen
Blanket's pink blanket!

"You can borrow my squeaky bone. It's pink like your blanket," said Champy.

"Thank you!"

Yummy!

SQUEAK!
went the bone

and surprised Blanket.

Parsnip tried to cheer up
Blanket. "Tadpole's found some
biscuits," he said. "They might
taste nice like your blanket."

"I have an idea," said Parsnip. "You can have my very special blue jumper. It's soft and cuddly like your blanket."

"Thank you!"

Parsnip helped Blanket pull on
the jumper . . .

"Help!" cried Blanket.
"Everybody, PULL!" said Parsnip.

The friends pulled
and pulled
until . . .

Whumph!

"Are you all right?"
asked Blanket.

"Thank you for helping me find it," said Blanket. "That's what friends are for," said Parsnip.

Other Toddler Books to collect:

Parsnip
Parsnip and the Runaway Tractor
Parsnip and the Sheep Game (coming soon)
by Sue Porter

Rory and the Lion
by Jane Cabrera

Grandma Rabbitty's Visit
by Barry Smith

What About Me?
by Helen Stephens